The
Snowman

Raymond Briggs

PUFFIN

HAMISH HAMILTON/PUFFIN

Penguin Books Ltd, 80 Strand, London WC2R 0RL, England
Penguin Putnam Inc, 375 Hudson Street, New York, New York 10014, USA
Penguin Books Australia Ltd, 250 Camberwell Road, Camberwell, Victoria 3124, Australia
Penguin Books Canada Ltd, 10 Alcorn Avenue, Toronto, Ontario, Canada, M4V 3B2
Penguin Books India (P) Ltd, 11 Community Centre, Panchsheel Park, New Delhi – 110 017, India
Penguin Books (NZ) Ltd, Cnr Rosedale and Airborne Roads, Albany, Auckland, New Zealand
Penguin Books (South Africa) (Pty) Ltd, 24 Sturdee Avenue, Rosebank 2196, South Africa

Penguin Books Ltd, Registered Offices: 80 Strand, London WC2R 0RL, England

First published by Hamish Hamilton Ltd 1978
Published in Puffin Books 1980

This edition published by Hamish Hamilton Ltd 1998
13 15 17 19 20 18 16 14 12

Published in Puffin Books 1998
29 30

Copyright © Raymond Briggs, 1978

Printed in Italy by Printers Trento Srl

British Library Cataloguing in Publication Data
A CIP catalogue record for this book is available from the British Library

ISBN 0-241- 13938-4 Hardback
ISBN 0-140- 50350-1 Paperback

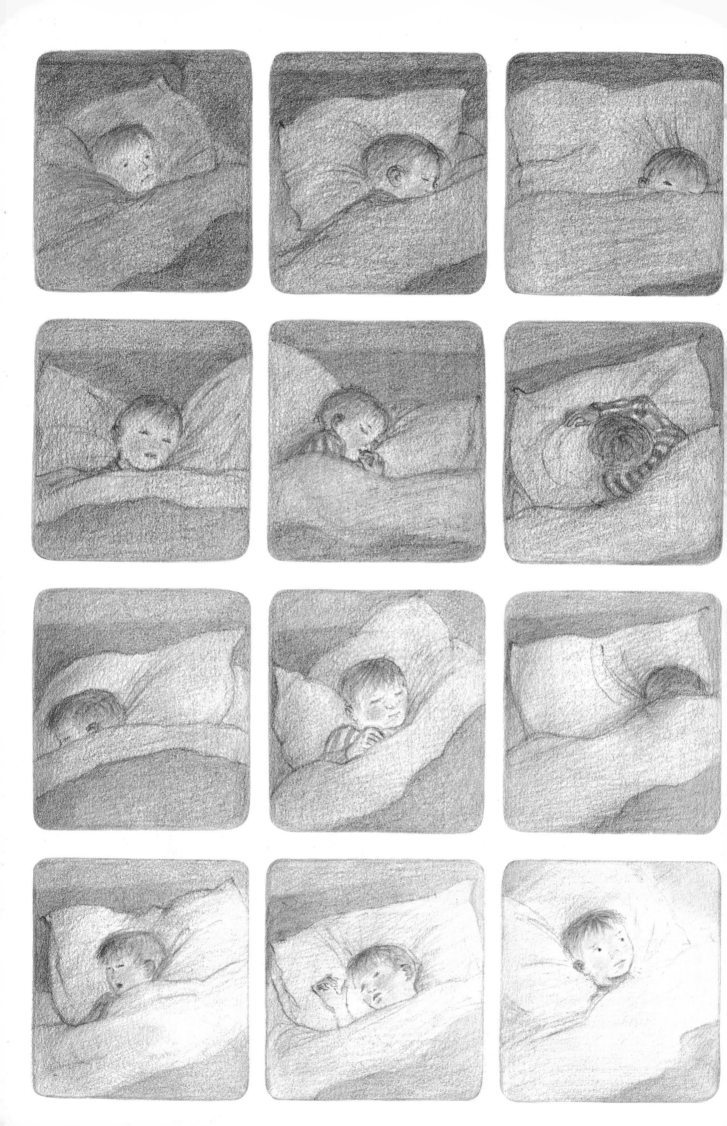

The Snowman is a beautifully illustrated picture book which has charmed children and adults for the last twenty years. Narrated entirely through pictures, it captures the innocence and wonder of childhood with its dreamlike illustrations. This unique book is a firm favourite all over the world and has become an intrinsic part of Christmas.

Some other Puffin picture books by Raymond Briggs:

THE SNOWMAN BOOK OF THE FILM
THE SNOWMAN STORYBOOK
FATHER CHRISTMAS
FATHER CHRISTMAS GOES ON HOLIDAY
JIM AND THE BEANSTALK
FUNGUS THE BOGEYMAN

PUFFIN

ISBN 0-14-050350-1

U.K.   £5.99
CAN $9.99

9 780140 503500